that's so raven

W9-BXT-977

Psyched

Adapted by James Ponti

Based on the television series, "That's So Raven", created by Michael Poryes and Susan Sherman

Part One is based on the episode written by Maria Espada

Part Two is based on the episode written by Michael Feldman & Jeff Abugov

Watch it on

DISNEY CHANNEL

abc Kids

DISNEY PRESS

VOLO

New York

Printed in the United States of America

First Edition
1 3 5 7 9 10 8 6 4 2

Library of Congress Control Number on file.

ISBN 0-7868-4693-3

For more Disney Press fun, visit www.disneybooks.com
Visit DisneyChannel.com

Part One

Chapter One

Raven Baxter and her best friends Eddie Thomas and Chelsea Daniels were walking down the halls of their school. It was almost first period or, as Raven liked to call it, six and a half hours till the bell rings.

"Hey, this is new," she said as she spotted a bottled-water vending machine.

Anything new was a surprise at Bayside, a place that took the term *old school* literally. Yeah, Raven thought, a little bottled water sounds pretty good right about now. Some H_2O for my get-up-and-go.

Then she saw the price. "A dollar for water? That's ridiculous."

Ridiculous—and exactly one dollar more

than she had. Raven turned to her friends. "Eddie, give me a dollar."

Typical, Eddie thought. She doesn't even ask. She just tells me to give her money.

"Broke again?" he asked.

"No," Raven said, rolling her eyes. "I just don't have change for a million."

To Raven, there were two types of people. Some—like her brother, Cory—had money, but wouldn't give her any. Others—like Chelsea and Eddie—were usually broke, so they couldn't give her any. Either way, she always suffered.

"Hey, the fountain's free," Chelsea said, always quick to point out the positive.

Right, Raven thought. And you get what you pay for.

Chelsea went to the fountain to get a drink, but all that came out of it was disgusting brown sludge. "No wonder there's never a line," she said as she fought the urge to gag.

Then, over the normal morning noise of lockers opening and closing and kids talking, Raven and her friends noticed something unusual—jazz.

"Where's that music coming from?" Eddie wondered.

Before Raven could turn to see, she froze in position. Rather than look down the hall, she saw straight into the future.

Through her eye
The vision runs
Flash of future
Here it comes—

I see a door—my front door.
The door cracks open and there are flowers. Wait, what's this? A boy carrying

flowers. Make that a really cute boy carrying flowers.

I don't recognize the boy. But he is definitely fine. This is looking good.

"Raven," he says as he holds out a bouquet of flowers. "These are for you."

Strike that. This is looking great.

Then the vision stopped. Dang, just when it was getting good, Raven thought. She even opened her eyes wider for an extra second, hoping to kick-start the vision into action again.

She didn't know who the boy was, but that wasn't going to stop her. She had to figure out a way to meet him.

"Hey, I know that face," Chelsea said, reading Raven's expression. "You just had a vision."

Raven smiled and nodded. "Chelsea, a

really cute guy came to my house, and he gave me flowers."

"Who was he?" Eddie wanted to know.

Chelsea had a more important question. "And does he have a friend?"

Raven scrunched her lip. "Well, I never saw him before . . ."

Just then the jazz started up again. A boy playing the sax was walking down the hall to class. Raven recognized him in a second—dark eyes, curly hair—it was the boy from her vision! Only this wasn't a vision—he was walking right past her. And he was just as fine in person.

". . . till this second," she continued. She turned to the musician and started to follow him. "Hey, cutie!"

"Oh, that's the new kid, Jonathan Kwizzowski," Eddie informed Raven and Chelsea. "They call him Kwizz. Anyway, he's totally into jazz."

"And I am totally into him," Raven added.

Raven could see it all. The sweet sounds of romance were in her future. There was just one problem.

"Now I just gotta meet him first," she said.

"How's it gonna happen?" asked Chelsea.

"That's the problem with these visions," Raven complained. "They show what you get but not how you get there." All she had seen was Kwizz at the door with flowers. She'd have to come up with a plan to make sure it happened.

"Oh my gosh," Chelsea blurted out. "The San Francisco Jazz Festival is next week. You should buy tickets and ask him out."

Now, that's a plan, Raven thought. Sometimes my girl really *does* help me out.

"Great plan," Eddie said. "Except she can't afford water."

That's cold, Raven thought. *True*, but still cold. Luckily, she had friends who loved her from the bottom of their hearts—and, she hoped, the bottom of their pockets.

"See, that's what friends are for. If we all dig down deep and—"

By the time she turned around to ask for money, Chelsea and Eddie were gone.

"Guys?" Raven called out. She realized it was useless. "I should've seen that coming."

Raven was not going to let her chance with Kwizz slip away. The jazz festival was the perfect idea. She just needed to come up with a quick source of income.

She thought for a moment, and a big, goofy smile flashed across her face. She knew just where to go.

Chapter Two

"**M**mmmm," Cory said, his mouth watering in anticipation as he sauntered into the kitchen the next morning. The table was piled high with so many delicious breakfast foods that he really had only one question. "Where to start?"

After some deep thought, he grabbed a blueberry muffin. He was just about to take a bite when Raven snatched it away. She knew just where he could start.

"With a box of cereal," Raven retorted. "'Cause all this," she said as she motioned to the table full of food, "not for you."

"Who's it for?" Cory asked.

"Mom and Dad," Raven explained. "They

get a gourmet breakfast, and all they have to do is sit through a short presentation about raising my allowance. Everybody wins."

She'd struck out with Chelsea and Eddie, but that was because she hadn't had a plan. Now she did. First she'd butter up some pancakes, and then she'd butter up her parents.

Raven had woken up early and cooked their favorites. If all went well, she'd have the money while the maple syrup was still hot. Then she'd be able to hit the jazz festival and make some sweet music of her own.

Cory had seen it all a million times. Didn't she know it was never gonna fly? "You could just come to me for money," he said. "I'm loaded."

"Yeah," Raven said, having already considered this. "But you always turn me down."

"And it never gets old," Cory said, flashing a great big smile. He was still laughing at his own joke when their parents walked into the kitchen.

Victor Baxter stopped cold and took a whiff. He was a professional chef, so it didn't take him long to figure out what was cooking. "Mmmm, smells like fresh blueberry muffins and hickory-smoked bacon," he said.

I am too cool for school, Raven thought. He's loving this breakfast thing. I wonder what I'll wear to the jazz festival?

Tanya Baxter surveyed the breakfast buffet. "Mmmm," she said skeptically. "Smells to me like we're getting hit up for cash."

Cory smiled at the sudden turn of events. But Raven hung tough. She had a plan and she was sticking to it. "Just hear me out," she urged, trying to sound as reasonable as she could.

She handed her parents a binder and began her presentation. At school, whenever she gave a presentation, she always imagined the rest of the class in their pajamas. That kept her from feeling uptight. But her parents actually were in their pajamas, so all she could do was plunge ahead.

"Okay, turn your attention to page eight," Raven said, trying to sound businesslike. "Now, as you know, I do my own clothes. I do my own nails. But I still need money for the essentials."

Both parents took a deep breath. There was no telling what Raven might consider "essential."

"We're talking hair, shoes, jazz festival tickets . . ."

She had tried to slip that last one in, but her father jumped on it. Hair and shoes he knew, but jazz was definitely out of the blue.

"Since when are you into jazz?" he asked.

"Like, forever, Daddy-O." Maybe some

jazz-speak would help her case, Raven thought. *"And all I need is the green to make the scene."*

Her dad wasn't buying it. *"I get what you're sayin', but I'm not payin',"* he replied.

Raven's mom got straight to the point. "Why don't you just save your money like your brother?" she asked.

Cory flashed a smile almost as big as his bank account. He loved these little moments.

"'Cause he's cheap," Raven explained, "and I've got a life."

"Which I can buy and sell," Cory answered, completely unfazed by the slam.

Raven was getting desperate. She tried that deep, pleading look she used when she wanted new shoes. It didn't matter. Her parents had already settled into their "not gonna happen" looks. This was one of those times when they were going to teach her a lesson.

"Baby," her mom said, "how are you ever going to learn the value of money if we just keep giving it to you?"

"By shopping?" Raven answered hopefully.

"No," said her dad. "By earning it. Do some extra chores. Get a part-time job."

A job? Raven thought. I hardly have time to be me. It takes work to look this good.

"I could use a foot massage," Cory remarked, putting his bare foot up on the table.

"You'd better get your little piggies away from my bacon," Raven's dad said as he shoved Cory's foot off the table.

Raven thought about what to do while her parents enjoyed their breakfast. She had no one else to ask for money. Maybe her dad was right. Maybe she did have to earn it. But no matter what, she needed a plan—and fast. The jazz festival was less than a week away.

* * *

That afternoon, Raven asked Chelsea and Eddie to come over to help her look for a job. They searched the want ads for anything that might put some quick cash into Raven's finely tailored pockets.

"Here's one, Rae!" Chelsea said hopefully. "'Lifeguard wanted.' It's perfect for you."

How long have this girl and I been friends? Raven wondered. "Hello! I cannot swim," she said.

"Well, if you're going to shoot down everything," Chelsea replied.

This was not going to be easy.

"Just keep looking, okay?" Raven pleaded. "There's got to be something out there. 'Cause I'm not letting this vision get away."

Raven couldn't believe how much trouble she was having. It wasn't like she was being greedy.

All she wanted was jazz festival tickets, a cute boy, flowers, and everlasting love. Was that too much to ask?

"Yo, check this one out," Eddie said. "PSYCHICS WANTED. EARN BIG BUCKS."

"Are you serious?" Raven asked.

"Right there," Eddie said, pointing to the ad in the paper. The job was for *Psychic Sidekicks,* a call-in TV show.

"I don't know," Raven said, looking worried. "Besides you guys and my family, no one else knows I'm psychic."

Chelsea nodded and added, "And, Rae, it's kinda wrong to use your powers, you know, to make money."

Raven thought about that for a moment. Maybe Chelsea was right. It *did* happen once in a while.

But Eddie didn't agree. "That's what gifts are for," he explained. He started to dribble an imaginary basketball. "You don't see Shaq just playing hoops in his driveway."

Raven nodded.

Next, Eddie moonwalked around the room. "And Michael Jackson doesn't just moonwalk around his pool."

Right again, Raven thought.

"And J.Lo. sure don't hide it in baggy pants," Eddie observed. He turned around and wiggled his rear end.

"I'm just saying," he continued, "if you've got it, you should use it."

Raven looked down at the ad. Maybe Eddie was right. Maybe this was the way to make that vision come true.

Chapter Three

When Raven got to the TV studio where *Psychic Sidekicks* was filmed, it was nothing like she'd imagined. There were lights everywhere, and it was really cold. What do they make here? she wondered. TV shows or ice cream sandwiches?

She tiptoed across the concrete floor so she wouldn't make any noise during the taping of the show.

"The cards tell me that you are very lonely," Madame Cassandra, the show's host was saying in a rich Jamaican accent.

"Yes," the caller said. "My man'll be gone for five to ten years."

Madame Cassandra looked into her crystal

ball for dramatic effect. "He's in jail, isn't he, child?" she asked.

"How did you know that?" the caller asked in amazement.

Madame Cassandra looked straight into the television camera. "If Madame Cassandra can't see it, it's not happenin'. Call me now!"

Just then the phone number for the show flashed on a TV monitor nearby.

Raven was impressed as she watched from behind the cameras. "Wow! She's amazing," she said to Hank Banks, the show's producer and the man interviewing her for the job.

"She's the best in the business," Mr. Banks said. "So, are you ready to be in the business?"

"Really?" Raven squealed. "I'm hired? Oh, thank you, Mr. Banks."

The "business" was what was going on behind her. There were dozens of phones ringing, each manned by a "psychic sidekick" who told the caller's fortune—for a price.

Now Raven was going to be one of them. Suddenly something dawned on her. Mr. Banks hadn't asked her if she was psychic. He must have forgotten.

"Don't you want to ask me some questions?" she asked.

"Are you a cop?" he asked.

Okay, that was not the interview question she'd been expecting. "No," Raven answered.

"Then no further questions," he said. He pointed at a phone on a nearby table. "Let's give it a whirl. This is where the magic happens."

Raven pulled up close so she could talk to him on the down low. "Listen, Mr. Banks," she said nervously. "You know, I've never really gone public about being psychic and everything.

"And plus, I don't even know when I'm

going to have my visions. Like the last one I had was about this really cute guy named Kwizz. He came to my door with these flowers, but he doesn't even really know I exist when I'm at school. So, I'm thinking about buying him these jazz concert tickets. . . ."

Raven noticed Mr. Banks had the same blank look her parents got when she babbled about her latest shopping jaunt.

"You don't care, do you?" she asked.

"Hey, you *are* psychic," he said with a smile. "Now, the name of the game is 'keep people on the line,' right? The more they talk, the more we make.

"So, if you think somebody's about to hang up," Mr. Banks asked, "what do you do?"

Raven pretended she was talking on a phone. "Thanks for calling?"

Mr. Banks was horrified. That was exactly what he didn't want her to say.

"No," he instructed. "You say, 'Wait, wait, I think I'm getting something.'" As he said this, he pretended to be experiencing a psychic event.

So, I'm just supposed to keep callers on the line even if I'm not getting a vision? Raven thought. That seems a little shady.

"I don't know," she said. "I mean, something doesn't feel right."

"Well," Mr. Banks said, "if you don't want fifteen bucks an hour—"

"Fifteen an hour?" Raven blurted, cutting him off. Food, clothes, jazz tickets. She had a lot of good uses for fifteen dollars an hour. Maybe she needed to reconsider. She might get visions while she was on the phone, and that would make it legit, right? "Wait! I think I'm getting something . . ." she said, putting her hands to her temples and pretending to have a vision.

Mr. Banks smiled and they shook on it. In an instant, Raven Baxter went from being a secret psychic junior high school student to full-fledged professional psychic sidekick.

At school on Monday morning, Raven decided it was time to land a sidekick of her own—Kwizz. She found him playing an incredible jazz solo for a group of students.

When he stopped for a beat, she tried to introduce herself. "Hi," she said. "My name is—"

Just then Kwizz blasted a couple of notes that made it impossible for him to hear her. The boy definitely had skills, Raven thought. She tried again. "So, how long have you—"

Again, she was drowned out by the sax. This time it was a long riff. Raven was getting anxious. She wanted to skip past the *solo* and go straight to the *duet*.

"You know, I got these tickets to the—" she offered.

Kwizz didn't hear a word she said. He was totally lost in his music. He blew a long note that seemed to last forever.

Frustrated, Raven grabbed a half-eaten banana from a girl next to her and stuck it into the bell of Kwizz's sax. By the time Kwizz caught on, she was already walking away. Chelsea and Eddie caught up to her.

"How am I gonna ask that boy to the jazz festival if he never stops playing?" she asked.

Eddie smiled. "Well, if you're talking about concert tickets," he said, "I'm guessing you got the job."

"Yeah, I got it," Raven said tentatively. She still wasn't sure if working at the Psychic Sidekicks Network was a good idea. Especially since it didn't seem to be getting her any closer to Kwizz.

"Oh my gosh, Rae, congratulations," said Chelsea excitedly. She jumped up and down, giving Raven a congratulatory bear hug. "Now you can use your psychic powers to make the world a better place."

Raven wasn't feeling it, though. Something about *Psychic Sidekicks* still didn't sit right with her.

"Uh, Rae, you're kinda bringing down the hug," Chelsea said, still hugging her and holding out for a response.

"Chels," Raven answered. "The job isn't exactly what you think it is."

Eddie nodded. "Yeah, but how's the money?"

"It's great," Raven answered. "But you don't even have to be a psychic. They'll hire anyone."

Chelsea and Eddie exchanged a look. "Great" money and "hire anyone" were all they needed to hear.

Chapter Four

"**Y**es, yes, wait, I'm getting something," Chelsea said as she spoke into a phone on the set of *Psychic Sidekicks*. She already had that line down cold. "Yes, it's a name. . . ." She paused. "Yes, and it starts with an *A*."

Chelsea waited for a response. "Okay, a *B*," she tried. Pretty soon, she was whipping through the alphabet. "You know, maybe it was a *C. D, E, F, G, H, I, J, K . . . J, J—J?*"

Finally, she got it.

"Yes, yes. I was actually going to say that first," she said as she tried to cover. "But I didn't want to freak you out."

Chelsea and Eddie were the newest Psychic Sidekicks. Unlike Raven, they had no problem pretending to be psychic. After all, they talked on the phone all the time. Why not get paid for it?

"Wait, I'm getting something," Raven said, knitting as she worked the phone next to Chelsea. "I see love in your future. . . ." She dragged it out to make it sound more mysterious. ". . . A nice . . . younger man," she ventured. She listened as the caller gave her the scoop. "You're ninety-four?" Raven blurted. "Well, everyone's younger than you, so I'm right."

Meanwhile, Eddie was working in a third cubicle. "Wait, hold on, I'm getting something," he said as he chomped on some chips. Getting a doughnut, that is, he said to himself as he grabbed one from a nearby box.

Chelsea was still trying to match the letter *J* with a full name. "Jim? Jason? Jenny?" she tried in vain. Finally, the caller gave up and told her.

"Jinxy? That's a cat's name," Chelsea said. "Oh, it *is* a cat. Yes."

While the young psychics fielded calls, Madame Cassandra was having an argument with the producer, Hank Banks.

"Oooo, Mr. Hank," she said, sounding as if she was talking to a caller. "Madame Cassandra see an ill wind a-blowin', and the spirits are a-cryin'."

"Get to the point, Shirley," Mr. Banks said. Madame Cassandra dropped the Jamaican accent. "I need a raise," she said bluntly.

"Forget it," Hank Banks shot back. "Grab your bag of bones and tighten your turban. 'Cause you're on in five minutes."

"Either I get my raise, you sleazebag, or I'm out of here," she threatened. "And this show would be nothing without Madame Cassandra."

"Are you kidding?" Mr. Banks responded. "Any of these clowns could replace you."

To illustrate his point, he turned to the phone bank to find a replacement for Madame Cassandra.

"Hey, hey, hey, you," he said to Eddie.

"Wha—" Eddie answered with a mouthful of doughnut.

Okay, maybe not Doughnut Boy, Mr. Banks thought. But one of the other kids could do it.

He turned to Chelsea. "You," he said.

But Chelsea was still trying to find her psychic groove. "Hi, Jinxy," she said into the telephone. "Who's a kitty? Meow, meow, meow."

Then Mr. Banks saw Raven. Perfect, he thought. Unlike her friends, she seems to have the psychic flair.

"You," he said to Raven. "You're my new star."

Minutes later, Raven was on the set, sitting in front of a "crystal ball." She had just gotten into costume: a sequined turban, a gold robe, and big hoop earrings—plus a pair of glasses so that no one would recognize her. Only someone with my sense of fashion could've put this together so quickly, Raven thought to herself.

Good-bye, Raven Baxter. Hello, Miss Tallulah, new star of the *Psychic Sidekicks* show.

She looked right into the camera as the show went on the air.

"Miss Tallulah on the line," Raven said in a Jamaican accent just like Madame Cassandra's. "Ready to tell your future. Next caller."

Raven pressed a button on the telephone next to her chair.

"Who be you?" she asked.

"My friends call me Kwizz," the caller said.

Doesn't that just figure, Raven thought. She'd been trying to talk to him all week at school. Now when she finally had the chance to make a love connection, she was pretending to be someone else.

"Kwizz," she said with a gulp, momentarily losing her accent.

Luckily, Kwizz started to explain his problem. "Well, I'm trying to get a scholarship to jazz camp this summer."

Suddenly, Raven realized that she could use this to her advantage. She looked into the crystal ball dramatically and pretended to conjure up an image. "You play the sax," Raven said.

"That's amazing. How'd you know?" Kwizz asked.

"Oh well, child, it's right here in my crystal ball." Raven picked up the ball for emphasis. For the first time she noticed that the ball was actually a souvenir snow globe from Washington, D.C. "And so is the Lincoln Memorial," she added under her breath.

"So, do you think I'll get the scholarship?" Kwizz asked desperately.

"Well, let's see, child," Raven said. She couldn't lie to Kwizz. She tried to stall. "What is your sign?"

"Aries," Kwizz answered.

"Ah, the fish," Raven said, hoping that was right. Just because she had visions didn't mean she paid attention to astrology.

"The ram," Kwizz corrected.

"I knew that," Raven said, trying to cover her mistake. "I was just ordering lunch." She looked off camera and pretended to give her lunch order. "I'll take the fish."

Suddenly, Raven felt a wave of psychic energy fill her body. Unlike her Miss Tallulah act, this vision was real.

**Through her eye
The vision runs
Flash of future
Here it comes—**

I see Kwizz. He's at home, sitting on his couch. Hmmm, I don't see myself sitting next to him. . . .

He's reading a letter to himself. After a few moments he smiles broadly.

"I got the scholarship!" he shouts.

Just as quickly as it had come, the psychic vision ended, leaving Raven a bit disoriented.

"Miss Tallulah?" Kwizz asked. "Are you there?"

"Yes, child, and with good news." Raven was thrilled that she didn't have to make something up. "Pack up your sax, Kwizz. You're going to jazz camp."

"Wow, thanks," Kwizz said, overjoyed. "Is there anything else?"

"Oh yeah, I hope so," Raven answered, hoping that there would be a lot more between them, just nothing else that involved *Psychic*

Sidekicks. Then she realized she had the perfect opportunity.

"I mean, wait, I think I'm getting something," she continued, putting her hands to her head. Behind the camera, Hank Banks gave her a big thumbs-up.

Raven sorted through a pile of chicken bones by the crystal ball. "Oh yes, child, the mystic bones are rattlin'," she said. "They say you must meet a girl."

"Who is she?" Kwizz asked, sounding desperate.

"Oh, child, she's at your school," Raven answered. "I see she's very, very beautiful, really. With a name like a bird."

"Robin?" Kwizz guessed.

"No," Raven retorted.

"Lark," he tried next.

"No," Raven answered, a little perturbed.

"Nancy Hawkstein?"

Raven couldn't believe it. How could he remember Nancy Hawkstein and not her? What did she need to do, run around with a sign?

"Forget it. Her name is Raven. You've got to go meet her. She lives at 519 Miranda Place. Ring her doorbell Friday night. Around, yes, the mystic says around eight."

"I don't get it," Kwizz said. "Why do I have to go to her—?"

"No backin'-talkin', child," Raven interrupted. "This is what the mystic says. It's the only way to get your scholarship. She's your good-luck charm."

From his place behind the camera, Mr. Banks signaled for Raven to wrap it up. She nodded.

"All right, thanks for calling, Kwizz," she said. Then she spoke to the viewers. "This is Miss Tallulah. Call me now. Call me sidekicks, because your future's on the line."

The stage manager signaled that they were off the air, and Mr. Banks rushed over to Raven.

"Wow!" he exclaimed. "That was great, kid. The phones are ringing off the hook. And the weird look that you get in your eyes . . ." He imitated the look Raven had gotten during her vision. ". . . keep it. It's gold."

When Mr. Banks left, Eddie and Chelsea came over to talk with Raven.

"So, what do you think of Miss Tallulah?" Raven asked.

"Um, I think she's using her powers to manipulate a guy into liking her," Chelsea answered, a little disappointed in her friend.

"Chels, okay, I just want to meet him," Raven replied.

"And then what?" Chelsea wanted to know.

"Well, you know," Raven answered. "Once

we're alone together, he'll realize we're meant for each other."

Chelsea gave her a disapproving look.

"Hey, I'm just trying to do what you're saying," Raven shot back. "Making the world a better place . . ." For emphasis, she used her new Jamaican accent. ". . . just one guy at a time, child."

Chapter Five

"**S**o, the kids are out and we have the house to ourselves," Mrs. Baxter remarked to her husband in a romantic tone. Time alone was rare for the two of them. "You know what that means?" she asked as she cuddled next to him.

"Oh, yeah," Mr. Baxter said.

Mrs. Baxter leaned in for a kiss at the exact moment that the doorbell rang.

"Pizza!" her husband said excitedly as he stood up and headed to the front door with visions of pepperonis dancing in his head.

So much for a romantic evening, Mrs. Baxter thought.

Mr. Baxter opened the door to reveal a delivery guy holding a large pizza box.

"That'll be twenty-two fifty," the man said.

"Cool," Mr. Baxter said as he dug through his pockets, looking for money. He was low on cash, just like his daughter. "Honey, I didn't get a chance to go to the ATM. Do you have any money on you?"

His wife shrugged. "I picked up the cleaning. I'm broke."

Mr. Baxter turned back to the pizza guy.

"Do you take credit cards?" he asked hopefully.

"Gee, let me check my shirt," the delivery guy answered sarcastically. He turned around to reveal CASH ONLY written on the back of his shirt.

Mr. Baxter really wanted the pizza. "There's gotta be some cash around here someplace," he told his wife.

They thought for a moment and smiled. There was one member of the Baxter family who always had plenty of money on hand. They ran upstairs.

"It's gotta be here someplace," Mrs. Baxter said as they entered Cory's room.

"Yeah, Cory's loaded," her husband added. "You know, he hasn't spent a dime of his birthday or Christmas money since he was born."

Mr. Baxter looked to see if any cash was hidden under Cory's mattress. Instead, he found something else. "Uh-oh, I found a magazine," he said.

Mrs. Baxter was not happy. "I blame you," she told her husband.

Then she saw the title. "*Retire at Twelve?*" she said. Oh good, she thought. It was a business magazine, nothing to worry about.

Just then, Mr. Baxter moved a framed poster of a basketball player. Behind it was a safe.

"Jackpot! Jackpot!" he said. "What do you think the combination is?"

Mrs. Baxter thought for a moment and had an idea. "Try his birthday."

Her husband nodded and typed in the numbers of Cory's birthday on the safe's keypad. It all seemed so simple.

"He's not so smart," Mr. Baxter said confidently.

Then the sound of an alarm filled the room. Steel bars slammed down from the ceiling, and red lights flashed. Within seconds, a net sprang down and pulled Mr. and Mrs. Baxter into midair.

As they swung in the net, Cory's face popped up on a video monitor.

"Attention, intruder," he said. "You have breached security in my room. Attention, intruder. You have breached security in my room."

"Why that little—" Mr. Baxter yelled as he tried to break free from the net.

Before Mr. Baxter could finish, Cory burst into the room, certain that he'd finally trapped his big sister. "I got you, Raven!" he cried gleefully. Then he noticed who was actually in the net. He couldn't believe his eyes.

"Mom? Dad?" he said. "I am so disappointed."

As if that wasn't bad enough, Mr. Baxter saw that Cory was already eating a slice of his pizza.

Friday night, Raven was getting ready for Kwizz to show up. She knew he'd take Miss Tallulah's advice and be at the Baxter house at eight. Then all it would take was a brief conversation for him to fall head over heels for her.

The doorbell rang and she smiled. She didn't need to be a psychic to know that something good was going to happen. She cracked open the door and poked her head out. Kwizz was standing there with flowers—just like in her vision.

"Raven?" he asked. "Like the bird?"

"Yes?" she answered. "And who are you?"

"It's Kwizz," he said. "From school."

"Kwizz, what are you doing here?" she asked, pretending to be surprised. This is almost too easy, she thought.

"I know this is going to sound kind of weird," he told her. "But, Raven, you're my good-luck charm."

"Oh?" Raven cooed. "That is the sweetest thing to say.

"You know what," she continued. "I really wasn't expecting company, but what the heck. Come on in."

Raven opened the door all the way, and Kwizz got his first look at her. She was wearing a gorgeous full-length silk dress. Let's see Nancy Hawkstein pull this off, she thought.

"Raven, these are for you," Kwizz said as he handed her the bouquet.

"Thank you," she replied graciously.

"That's a nice dress you've got there," he continued.

"This old thing? Darling, I made it this morning," she said.

It all was coming together perfectly—Kwizz, the flowers, the dress. The jazz festival was going to be amazing. But then something happened that Raven hadn't foreseen.

"Lisa, check this out," Kwizz called out the door.

"Lisa?" Raven asked, suddenly confused and more than a little worried.

A pretty girl entered the room. She hadn't been part of the vision. And she was definitely not part of Raven's plan.

"Lisa," Kwizz said to the girl, "Raven made this dress all by herself."

Lisa looked at the dress admiringly. But before she could reply, Raven tried to redirect things.

"Yes, girl," Raven explained. "And we are so excited about it." To emphasize which "we" she meant, Raven pointed to Kwizz and herself. "But who are you?"

"Oh, sorry," Kwizz said. "This is my girlfriend."

Raven was crushed. "Lisa," she said, barely able to spit the name out.

"I had to meet Kwizz's good-luck charm," Lisa explained. As she spoke, she looped her hand through Kwizz's arm.

"You have a girlfriend?" Raven asked Kwizz one last time.

"Yeah. Yeah, I do," he explained. "So I came to your house. I met you. I gave you the flowers—it was Lisa's idea."

Raven shook her head. She couldn't believe it.

"Lisa," she said again. The whole having-a-girlfriend thing was still sinking in.

"Well, it was nice meeting you," Lisa said.

"Yeah, yes it was," Raven said politely. Chelsea had been right. She'd tried to use her psychic powers to make a guy like her. It had been wrong. And now she was paying the price.

"It's funny how things work out. . . . Or don't," Raven said to herself.

Raven picked up a pair of tickets from the table and handed them to Kwizz. "Here, you guys might like these," she said.

"Tickets to the jazz festival," Kwizz blurted. "You really are my good-luck charm."

Kwizz held out his hand, hoping for a high five. Raven looked at it for a moment. She had hoped to be holding that hand at the festival, not giving it a high five. But she didn't want to leave him hanging, so she slapped it.

Raven watched Kwizz and Lisa go and then sat down, totally dejected. Sometimes the problem with her visions was that you didn't know what happened right before them. But now she realized that what happened right afterward was sometimes even worse.

Chapter Six

"Oh, man, he had a girlfriend?" Chelsea asked the next day at work.

"Lisa," Raven retorted. "You were right, Chels. I shouldn't have used my gift to get a guy."

"Yeah," Eddie added. "And I shouldn't have filled up on doughnuts when they're bringing in the deli platter."

Chelsea tried to be encouraging. "Rae, I don't know. Maybe you should look on the bright side. You know, at least no one got hurt."

Girl, did you even hear what I said? Raven thought.

"But *me*," Raven said.

"There you go," Chelsea said, missing the point. "Bright side!"

Mr. Banks came over to them. He pointed right at Eddie and Chelsea. "Hey, you two. Back on the phones. Let's go."

Chelsea and Eddie went back to their cubicles, and Mr. Banks turned to Raven.

"Okay, you. You're on," he said.

Just then Mr. Banks noticed something unusual. Chelsea wasn't answering a call. She was dialing out to make one.

"Hi, Doris, it's Chelsea, your psychic sidekick," she said into her headset. "How's little Jinxy doing? Still hacking out that hairball? Wow!"

Mr. Banks couldn't believe it. "Hold it. First of all, we don't make money when the psychics call the customers," he barked at Chelsea. "And second of all, you're fired. And take Jaws with you."

Mr. Banks motioned to the next cubicle, where Eddie had his mouth open wide, ready to chomp down on a gigantic sandwich.

Eddie and Chelsea shrugged. Losing the job was not a big deal. After all, it wasn't like they were real psychics. Still, they decided to hang out and watch Raven.

Dressed as Miss Tallulah, Raven took her spot in front of the camera. Her mind was still focused on Kwizz when the first viewer called.

"Okay, caller," she said, using her phony Jamaican accent. "Who be you?"

"This is Kwizz again," the caller said. Raven couldn't believe it.

"What's wrong, Kwizz?" she asked.

"I didn't get into jazz camp," he said. "I was supposed to hear by now."

Raven was certain that he was getting in. After all, her visions were always right, even if she didn't know when they were going to happen.

"The mail's a little slow, child," she said, trying to sound reassuring. "No reason to get your horn out of tune."

Kwizz wasn't so sure. "I must've messed things up with Raven," he explained. "Maybe I shouldn't have brought my girlfriend."

You are so right about that, Raven thought.

"Well, I can't argue with you there, child," she said.

"Wait, wait, what are you saying?" Kwizz asked. "Should I break up with her?"

Raven realized that she had to be straight with Kwizz. She couldn't use her gift—or her spot on the *Psychic Sidekicks* television show— to get a guy to dump his girlfriend. It just wasn't right.

"Whoa, no. No, Kwizz, no," she instructed. "That would be bad. We don't want nobody to get hurt because of what Miss Tallulah say."

"Miss Tallulah, I'm freaking out," Kwizz responded. "How come I didn't get that scholarship? Am I jinxed? Did I lose my talent? Should I quit music?"

"Kwizz, no, you're wrong, child," Raven answered. "Take the island breath. No one play the horn like you. And you don't need to call Miss Tallulah to tell you that."

Mr. Banks looked up from his sandwich. "Yes, he does," he said in total disbelief.

Just then Madame Cassandra came up behind him. She could tell that he was starting to get worried about what was happening on the show. "So, any clown can do this, huh, Hank?" she asked.

Meanwhile, Raven was still trying to set the record straight with Kwizz. "Listen to Miss Tallulah," she said. "Okay, you're wasting your money calling me."

"No he's not," Mr. Banks shouted, about to

blow his top. "What is she saying?" he asked desperately.

Madame Cassandra saw her chance. "So, how about that raise?" she asked.

"Fine, anything," Mr. Banks answered. "Just get out there and keep that kid on the line."

Meanwhile, Kwizz was getting more desperate by the minute.

"Please, Miss Tallulah," he pleaded. "Check the mystic bones. What do they say?"

Raven couldn't believe how much he bought into all of this psychic mumbo jumbo. The boy could play some notes but was a little slow to pick up signals.

"Kwizz, Kwizz, Kwizz," she shouted to get his attention. "Listen, these are not mystic bones." She reached under the table and pulled out a bucket from a fried-chicken joint. "Child, this was my lunch. Okay, it's a secret recipe and very good, but there's nothing mystical about it."

"Are you saying you're not a real psychic?" Kwizz asked her.

"Well, that's a complicated question," Raven answered honestly.

Before she could explain that she actually was a psychic but the television show was fake, Madame Cassandra came onto the set.

"Ooooh, de spirits," she said with great Caribbean flair. "Dey are very angry."

"Madame Cassandra?" Raven blurted, surprised to see her.

"Dey're saying she lies, Kwizz!" Madame Cassandra said to the camera. "Like a Jamaican dog full of sand fleas!"

She turned to Raven and said forcefully, "Now get out!" Then she turned back to the camera and smiled as though everything was going to be okay. "Kwizz, stay on the line."

"Listen to me, Kwizz," Raven said, not

moving an inch. "No real psychic would ever be on a cheesy show like this."

"Oooo, you hear that?" Madame Cassandra said to the camera. "She's a bad coconut. Excuse me while I shake the evil out of her."

Madame Cassandra grabbed Raven by the arms and shook her while the people on the set gathered around to watch. Raven wriggled away and taunted Madame Cassandra.

"Missed me."

Then Madame Cassandra grabbed at Raven's turban. "Gotcha!" she yelled. As she pulled on the turban, it unwound and spun Raven around in a circle.

"Okay, that's enough," Raven said. "Getting dizzy. Here comes lunch."

"Say toodle-oo, Tallulah," Madame Cassandra said.

Raven had had enough. She pulled the last

of the turban off her hair and grabbed a finger from a giant Styrofoam hand that was used as a prop.

"Bring it on, Shirley," she said, using Madame Cassandra's real name.

"Oh, snap. No, you didn't just break my hand!" Madame Cassandra said, her fake accent long gone.

"What are you gonna do about it?" Raven challenged.

Madame Cassandra broke off another finger and got ready to fight.

"Oh, I guess you could do that," Raven gulped, worried that maybe she was in over her head. Still, she fought back, and the two had a giant-finger duel around the set, wielding the props as if they were in a sword fight.

"Rae sure swings a pretty mean finger, doesn't she?" Eddie remarked proudly to Chelsea.

While she was fighting, Raven turned to the

camera and called out to Kwizz. "Hang up, Kwizz!"

"Wait, wait, wait. I think I'm getting something," Madame Cassandra said, trying to keep him on the line.

"Yeah," Raven said, seeing her opportunity. "You're getting this!"

Raven knocked the giant finger out of Madame Cassandra's hand and backed her up against a table so that she couldn't fight back.

"Hey, I don't need this," Madame Cassandra said. "I made more money waitressing."

"Am I getting charged for this?" Kwizz said into the phone. "'Cause nobody's helping me!"

"Kwizz, don't you see?" Raven said. "It's all a fake."

Raven took off her prop glasses. Now without these and the turban, she no longer looked like Miss Tallulah.

"Look," she said into the camera. "Hello, it's me. Raven!"

"Wait," Kwizz shouted back, distracted. "The mail just came!"

On the other end of the phone, Kwizz was opening an envelope.

"I got the scholarship!" he shouted. "Well, I'd better call Lisa!"

Kwizz hung up the phone.

Back at the *Psychic Sidekicks* set, Raven couldn't believe it. She turned to Madame Cassandra, who was still pinned against the table.

"Did you see that?" Raven complained. "He still didn't notice me."

"Just like a man," Madame Cassandra said knowingly.

"That's right," Raven remarked, and helped her up. Together they walked over to Mr. Banks, who looked stunned by what he'd just seen.

"Hank," Raven said, "I think you're out of business."

"Are you kidding?" Hank Banks answered. "You gave me a great idea."

Raven and Madame Cassandra looked at each other, too puzzled for words.

"Female Psychic Gladiators," he explained. "It's going to be huge."

"Really?" Chelsea interrupted. "Does it pay a lot? Because I'm going to need a summer job."

Raven and Eddie pulled her away. One television show had been quite enough. It was time to leave—for good.

At school on Monday, Raven looked at the new vending machine. Eddie was there, searching his pockets for some cash.

"Yo, Rae, got a buck?" he asked.

Raven shook her head. "I'm busted," she explained.

"Again?" Eddie asked. "I was counting on you treating for the movies tonight."

Raven couldn't believe it. "Well, I was counting on you," she said.

Eddie had seen it all before. He looked at Raven and sighed. "I guess everybody's broke then."

Then an idea occurred to Raven. "Not everybody," she answered mischievously.

That afternoon, Raven snuck into her brother's bedroom and went straight for the safe.

She flashed a devilish smile as she punched a combination into the keypad. The smile didn't last long. Within seconds, an alarm sounded, steel bars blocked the window, and Raven was suspended in midair by a giant net.

She fought and struggled, but it was no use. He had her cold. "Cory!" she called out in disgust. "Get me out of here."

Cory walked into the room, shaking his head. He acted as though he was disappointed in Raven, but he couldn't have been happier. He'd finally trapped his nemesis.

Cory took a refreshing sip from a bottle of water. "They'll never learn," he said as his sister swung above him, unable to do a thing about it.

that'sSO
raven

Part Two

Chapter One

The gymnasium at Bayside was jammed to the roof with screaming fans as the Bayside volleyball team battled Jefferson in the biggest match of the year. Jefferson led the game 14–13 and was only one point away from winning for the twenty-eighth year in a row.

"We've gotta stop this next play," Eddie said to the girl next to him. "Or those scrubs from Jefferson are going to beat us again!"

"I'm a scrub from Jefferson," the girl said.

Eddie took a good look at her and considered his options. "Go, Jefferson," he cheered. "Get busy!" School spirit was one thing, but this girl was cute.

Just then a Jefferson player hit the ball over

the net. Raven was in the center of the Bayside front line and had the best play on the ball.

"I got it! I got it!" she shouted.

This was her chance to stop Jefferson's winning streak, her moment of glory. She could see a future filled with adoring fans, magazine covers, and commercial endorsements. Then she was overcome by a vision.

Through her eye
The vision runs
Flash of future
Here it comes—

I see Chelsea, standing by a table. Something's wrong. Oh no, I hope my girl is okay. Chelsea lifts her hand.

"Oooo," Chelsea says. "I broke a nail."

Just as Raven came out of the vision, the volleyball flew over the net and bonked her right on the head. It bounced off and landed on the floor. Game over. Jefferson had won—again.

The Jefferson fans cheered while the now-quiet Bayside fans exited. Chelsea walked over to Raven to check on her.

"Rae, what happened?" she asked. "You said you had it."

Raven turned so that only her friend could hear her. "Yeah, I did. But then I had a vision," she said. She motioned to the team. "Chels, do you think they're mad?"

Raven and Chelsea looked over at the rest of the team. There was not a friendly face in the pack.

"It's cool, Rae," Chelsea said nonchalantly. "I'll handle it."

As the teammates crowded around the two friends, Chelsea tried to explain. "Now, I know what you're thinking," she said. "This was our championship game and Raven blew our one shot at beating Jefferson after twenty-seven years—"

"Chels," Raven tried to interrupt. So far, she didn't seem to be helping Raven's case. But Chelsea was determined.

"I got it, Rae," she said confidently. Then she turned to the rest of the team and continued, "Twenty-seven long years—"

"Chelsea!" Raven barked, cutting her friend off.

Raven turned to her teammates and said the only thing she could. "I'm sorry, you guys."

Her teammates just looked at her for a moment and walked off, still grumbling. Just then, Eddie came over and threw a friendly arm around Raven's shoulder.

"Yo, Rae," he said, somewhat comfortingly. "What happened out there?"

"She had a vision," Chelsea replied. "But it's cool 'cause I handled it."

Raven gave her a look. Handled it? Sometimes that girl was so clueless. But Raven was too upset to correct her.

"Well, I hope that was one important vision," Eddie responded. "Because twenty-seven years—"

"I know," Raven interrupted. It was going to be a while before people stopped mentioning the whole twenty-seven-year thing.

"So, what was it?" Eddie asked, curious about the vision.

Raven didn't want to answer. She couldn't control her visions. It wasn't her fault they were about little things sometimes. But that still didn't make her want to talk about this one.

"Chelsea's going to break a nail," she said sheepishly.

Chelsea and Eddie waited to see if she was joking. A broken nail? They'd lost the game over a broken nail? They couldn't believe it.

Raven tried to make it sound more important. "It was the pinkie," she explained. "Come on, you know the one she used to do Dr. Evil with?" Raven held up a crooked finger just like Dr. Evil in the Austin Powers movies. Raven's friends just stared at her.

"Hey, I didn't ask for these visions," Raven complained.

Eddie and Chelsea thought it over. Of course she was right. Anyway, they couldn't stay mad at her.

"It's cool," Chelsea said, with a warm smile. "Come on, let's get something to eat."

"Yeah," Eddie added. "We can celebrate . . ." Chelsea and Raven stared at him blankly. He paused, trying to come up with something. ". . . the fact that we all have our health."

"No, it's cool," Raven said, not in the mood to celebrate anything. "I'm just going to head home. But we're still on for bowling tomorrow, right?"

Chelsea and Eddie nodded.

"Bye, Rae," Chelsea said as they headed for the exit.

"Bye. Peace," Eddie added.

Just as Raven started to leave, the Jefferson girl Eddie had been flirting with walked up to her. "I know what happened to you out there," she said.

"Yeah," Raven answered. "I missed the ball."

The girl gave her a look. "But I know why." She reached into her pocket and pulled out a business card, which she gave to Raven.

Raven read it slowly. "'Sleevemore Center for Psychic Research'?"

"My name is Carly," the girl said. "Drop by sometime."

As Carly walked away, Raven looked down

at the card again. If Carly was a psychic, maybe she really did know what had happened.

Then it dawned on Raven. Maybe there were people like her out there after all.

Chapter Two

Raven's visions usually gave her a glimpse of the future, but she had no idea what was in store at the Sleevemore Center for Psychic Research.

Just as she was about to ring the doorbell later that afternoon, a boy opened the door as though he'd been expecting her.

"Hi, I'm looking for the—"

"This is it," he answered before Raven could finish.

Suddenly it dawned on her. He was probably reading her mind. "Oh, good," she continued. "Um, the reason I'm here . . ."

The boy touched his temples as if he was receiving some extrasensory communication.

"I know. I know," he said, again before she finished. "Volleyball, you had a vision, screwed up, everybody's mad at you, blah-blah-blah."

This kid was incredible. "Did you just read my mind?" Raven asked him.

"Well . . ." the boy said modestly.

Just then, Carly walked up and said, "Marvin, don't freak her out." Then she turned to Raven and explained, "I told him the whole story."

Raven shot Marvin a look, but he just smiled and said, "Gotcha."

Carly shook her head. She'd seen it before countless times. "Marvin's a second-degree telepath," she explained. "And a first-degree pain in the butt."

Marvin didn't seem offended at all. "That's why I love it here," he said. "In school, I'm just a pain in the butt."

Carly stepped between them. "You'll learn

to ignore him," she promised Raven as she escorted her inside. "Come on, I'll show you around."

Raven was still worried. Until the volleyball game, the only people who had known she was psychic were her family and her two closest friends. Now an entire group of strangers was going to find out. Part of her wanted to run away. But an even bigger part wanted to find out what it was like at the Sleevemore Center.

As she followed Carly inside, Raven couldn't believe what she saw. It was a laboratory filled with panels of blinking lights and gauges. A bunch of kids were working on various experiments as scientific equipment beeped and buzzed away.

"Ooh, your all's electric bill must be ridiculous!" Raven exclaimed. "What do you do here?"

"Well, we develop our psychic skills," Carly

explained. "Like Marlo here." Carly motioned to a girl sitting at a table. "She's a spoon bender."

Raven watched in amazement as Marlo stared at a spoon. Within seconds, the spoon started to bend from the force of Marlo's mental strength.

"Wow! You bend, girl," Raven cheered.

"We keep her away from the good silver," Carly assured her.

Next Raven noticed a redheaded boy who was staring at a marshmallow that a lab technician was holding with a long pair of tongs.

"And that guy there," Carly said, "can start fires with his mind. Hey, Sparky."

To Raven's untrained eye Sparky just seemed to be looking at a marshmallow. "So, what are they doing?" she asked. "Some kind of experiment?"

"No," Carly answered. "Actually, he's making s'mores."

Suddenly the marshmallow burst into flames. Sparky smiled, proud of what he'd done and eager for a snack.

That did not just happen, Raven thought. Is this for real? She turned to the others. "Did you see that marshmallow? And then, and then it . . . poof!" She couldn't believe no one else was as excited as she was.

"Am I the only one who thinks that's amazing?" she asked, loud enough for everyone to hear.

No one responded.

"Well," Raven said. "I guess I am. Okay."

"I guess we're just used to it," Carly explained.

Suddenly Raven looked at Carly and wondered what her gift was.

"So, what's your thing?" Raven asked her.

"Well, I'm a telepath. I can hear people's thoughts," she said. "And I'm telekinetic."

Raven had no idea what that was, but she liked the sound of it. "Oh," she said. "What's that?"

Carly pointed at an orange ball. As she moved her finger up, the ball floated off the table it had been sitting on. When Carly pointed downward, the ball floated back down to the table.

Raven was stunned but tried to play it cool. "Yeah," she said breezily. "But can you do the Shake?"

Raven showed off a couple of dance moves and did the Shake for a moment.

"You're going to fit right in," Carly assured her.

Raven wasn't so certain. "I don't really know," she confessed. "I mean, everybody

"I could use a foot massage," Cory remarked.

"Yo, check this one out," Eddie said.
"PSYCHICS WANTED. EARN BIG BUCKS."

"Really?" Raven squealed. "I'm hired?"

"Uh, Rae, you're kinda bringing down the hug," Chelsea said, still hugging her and holding out for a response.

"Miss Tallulah on the line," Raven said
in a Jamaican accent.

A net sprang down and pulled Mr. and
Mrs. Baxter into midair.

"You have a girlfriend?" Raven asked Kwizz one last time.

"Bring it on, Shirley," Raven said.

"Chels, do you think they're mad?" Raven asked.

The needle in the oscillator zigged and
zagged, and sparks flew from the helmet.

"You know how sometimes my visions can be a problem?" Raven asked.

"Ooh, smells like love, huh, Lionel?" Cory said.

"Tell me I did not just see that,"
Eddie said, totally amazed.

"We are gathered here today to join this couple in
holy matrimony," Cory said, completely serious.

"We come in peace," Chelsea announced.

"Okay," Raven shouted nervously.
"Who turned off the gravity?"

seems so in tune with their psychic abilities. I wish I was."

Suddenly she heard a man's voice behind her. "Then you've come to the right place."

Raven turned to see a friendly-looking scientist. He wore a long lab coat and a wide smile. "I'm Dr. Sleevemore," he said. "Welcome to my center."

Carly handled the introduction. "Dr. Sleevemore, this is Raven, the girl I told you about."

"Ah, Raven," he said knowingly. "You had the vision. Screwed up the volleyball game."

Raven was getting tired of everybody reminding her of the volleyball game. She turned to Carly and asked, "Did you have to tell everyone?"

"Carly didn't tell me," Dr. Sleevemore assured her.

"You read my mind?" Raven asked, impressed.

"No," he said with a laugh. "Marvin told me."

"Hey," Marvin protested.

"Good old Marvin," Raven said.

Dr. Sleevemore looked at her kindly. "Raven," he said. "I believe we can help you."

"Really?" Suddenly, Raven felt as if a huge burden had been lifted. For the first time, she had told people she didn't know about her psychic powers. Not only had they accepted her, but they wanted to help.

"First we measure your psychic abilities on the Sleevemore Cerebral Oscillator," Dr. Sleevemore said. He patted a bizarre-looking piece of machinery with a metal helmet that had tons of wires sticking out of it.

"The cerebral oscillator," Raven said. Then she thought of something. "Wait a second. Is that going to jack up my hair?"

"Oh, yes," he said.

Raven didn't like anyone messing with her hair. But maybe this test would help her figure out some stuff about herself. Besides, she always had a spare hat ready for emergency accessorizing.

Chapter Three

While Raven was busy becoming a lab rat, her brother, Cory, was concerned about an actual rat—his pet, Lionel.

"I'm worried about Lionel," Cory said to his parents as he walked into the kitchen holding his pet. Cory's mom looked up from her laptop.

"What's wrong?" she asked.

"I think he's lonely," Cory explained. "Can we get him a dog?"

Mr. Baxter stopped cooking for a moment. "You don't get a rat a dog," he explained.

"Victor," Mrs. Baxter called to her husband. "Lionel's not a rat!"

"Maybe he needs a girlfriend," Cory suggested.

"Whoa," Mr. Baxter said. "The last thing we need in this house is two rats. Why don't you get him a mirror?"

"Now, Victor," Mrs. Baxter said. "Every man needs a good woman in his life."

"Forget it," Mr. Baxter told Cory. "Get him a piece of cheese and he'll be just as happy."

Mrs. Baxter took this as a dig against her. "So you're equating cheese with the love of a good woman?"

Mr. Baxter opened his mouth to say something and thought better of it. He'd realized his mistake just a moment too late.

"You're going to turn this into something, aren't you?" he asked.

She gave him a look that said he'd better get with the program. Then she turned to her son. "Now, Cory, honey," she said. "Lionel's a part of the family, too. If you think he needs a lady friend, then we'll get him one."

Cory smiled. "Come on, Lionel," he said as he headed out the door. "Let's see if we can make a player out of you."

Mr. Baxter knew how crazy his son could get. There was no telling what he'd do to help Lionel get ready for his date. "Stay away from my aftershave!" he called to Cory.

Back at the Sleevemore Center, Raven was sitting in the chair of Dr. Sleevemore's cerebral oscillator. She was wearing the metal helmet, which seemed to be hooked up to all kinds of gauges and meters. All the other kids in the lab stared at her while the doctor tested her psychic ability.

Raven was trying to use her powers to "see" the image on the other side of the cards that Carly was holding.

"Circle?" she guessed hopefully.

"No," Carly said, looking down at the

star shape on the card. "Wrong again."

The others shook their heads. You didn't have to be a mind reader to tell that they all were thinking the same thing—Raven wasn't psychic at all.

"Looks like they're letting anyone in these days," Marvin whispered to Sparky.

"Marvin!" Dr. Sleevemore snapped. "Do we have to give you another time-out?"

Marvin shook his head and quieted down.

"Just relax, Raven," Dr. Sleevemore said in a comforting tone.

"You know, I'm not much of a card reader," Raven explained. "I'm more of a future seer."

"Ah, a clairvoyant," the doctor said.

"But I can't really just turn my visions on and off," she continued.

"Well, we know you can't turn them on," said Marvin with a snicker.

Raven gave him a look. "I think I'm seeing a long life of loneliness for you, Marvin," she said.

Dr. Sleevemore smiled. It didn't take a psychic to figure that out. "I'll tell you what, Raven," Dr. Sleevemore said gently. "Let's do this another day."

Just as he reached over to turn off the machine, Raven had a vision. As the psychic images went through her brain, surges of power and energy shot through the machinery. The lights flickered on and off. The needle in the oscillator gauge zigged and zagged, and sparks flew from the helmet.

"Dr. Sleevemore," Carly called. "It's oscillating."

"That's what oscillators do, Carly," he answered with a hint of excitement.

An instant later, Raven snapped out of her trance and the oscillator returned to normal.

"You just had a vision, didn't you?" Dr. Sleevemore asked excitedly.

"Yes," Raven answered. "And I suggest you take three steps to your left."

Dr. Sleevemore didn't know what to make of that, but he wasn't going to waste time trying to figure it out. He quickly moved three steps to his left. As soon as he did, a huge light fixture fell from the ceiling and crashed onto the floor, right where he had been standing.

The others gasped in amazement. Even for this crowd, Raven's vision had been impressive. They burst into applause.

"Good show, Raven," Dr. Sleevemore said. "You just registered a four-point-seven on the Sleevemore Psychic Scale." He paused for a moment and added, "And a perfect ten on the Sleevemore thank-you scale."

"Well, you know," Raven said modestly, "you should see me when I'm warmed up."

Marvin walked over to her. "I have to admit, I had my doubts," he conceded. "But you're definitely one of us."

"Welcome aboard," added Carly.

Raven was truly happy as the others came over and congratulated her. She felt as if she really fit in.

"Thank you. Oh my goodness. This is so weird," she admitted. "Normally, I have to hide my visions. But it's great to just be myself."

"Well, you're welcome to be yourself here anytime," Dr. Sleevemore assured her. "We meet again tomorrow."

"Okay," Raven said.

"And afterward," Marvin added, "we all go out for pizza."

Suddenly, Raven remembered her bowling date with Eddie and Chelsea. "Um, well, I kind of had something planned," she stammered. Then again, she always hung out with Eddie and Chelsea. It wouldn't be that big a deal to chill with some other kids for one night, would it? "But . . . you know what . . . never mind."

"Excellent," Dr. Sleevemore said. Just then he noticed a scent. "Ooh, I smell popcorn."

Raven looked across the room and saw that Sparky was using his powers to heat up a package of instant popcorn. After a few moments, the sound of popping kernels filled the room.

Raven smiled and joined the others as they gathered around Sparky.

Chapter Four

"**H**ey, Rae," Eddie said as he and Chelsea walked into Raven's room the next morning.

Raven was surfing the Net and was not happy with what she'd found. "Guys, did you see what they put on the school Web site? Look."

It was a replay of Raven losing the volleyball match. The highlight—or rather lowlight—kept playing again and again. Each time the ball hit her, there was a little *boink* sound effect. Chelsea and Eddie burst out laughing.

Raven scolded them. "It is *so* not that funny."

Chelsea and Eddie tried to keep it under control and look serious.

"Shameful," Eddie said.

"I'm completely not laughing," added Chelsea.

Raven couldn't believe it. It was bad enough that everybody in the gym had seen her blow the match, but now it was on the Web for the whole world to see.

Eddie quickly tried to change the subject. "So, Rae, where were you last night? I mean, I called to see how you were doing, but all I got was your machine."

"Well, you know, actually I was out. And I really wanted to talk to you about it," Raven started to explain. She wanted to tell her friends about the Sleevemore Center. "You know how my visions can sometimes be a problem—"

"Sometimes?" Chelsea interrupted. "Come here. May I direct you to the screen?" Chelsea pointed to the computer monitor and the game footage.

"Yeah, funny," Raven said, hurt by her friend's insensitivity.

"Man," Eddie added, "when you get that vision look on your face that . . ." Eddie started to imitate what Raven's face looked like when she had one of her visions. He was just kidding around, but Raven started to get upset.

Chelsea kept piling it on. "It's always something just really earth-shattering," she continued. "Like a broken nail."

She held up her pinkie like Dr. Evil. "By the way, Raven," she added. "Me and Pinkie, still waiting."

Raven couldn't believe her best friends were treating her like this. Suddenly she wished she were at the psychic center. No one there gave her flack about her visions.

"So, what did you want to tell us?" Eddie asked.

Raven thought for a moment. Why should she tell Eddie and Chelsea about the center? They'd probably make fun of her even more. "Just that I'm not gonna be able to go bowling with you guys tonight," she answered.

"Oh, no, C'mon, Rae," Chelsea said enthusiastically. "It'll be so much fun. We'll eat greasy food. Wear other people's shoes."

Raven thought about it. Normally, she would have loved to go bowling. But tonight she'd rather be with the kids from the center. Still, she couldn't tell Chelsea and Eddie that. She didn't want to hurt their feelings even though they'd hurt hers.

"I really can't make it," she explained, trying to think of an excuse. "You see, the thing is . . . Cory's rat is having this whole crisis, and you know how I like to be there for him.

"The rat," she corrected. "Not Cory."

"Okay, Rae, if you're sure," Chelsea said, a

little surprised that she'd choose time with a rat over bowling with them.

"I'm sure," Raven answered.

Cory's rat *was* having a crisis, but Raven wasn't about to help. Anyway, Cory had it under control. He had turned the entire living room into a rodent dating center. There were a dozen cages spread around the room, each holding a potential girlfriend for Lionel.

"Okay, who ordered the cheddar?" Mrs. Baxter said as she entered the room, carrying a plate filled with cheese cubes. She put a cube in each of the cages.

Mr. Baxter walked into the room. He couldn't believe his eyes. Living with one rat had been bad enough. This was out of control.

"What is this, a rat motel?" he asked. "Okay, everybody, checkout time! Move your tails!"

"Victor, stop it," Mrs. Baxter said. She

thought Cory had it right, and she was going to help make Lionel happy. "The rats are here because we put up a flier in the pet store. Their owners brought them over."

"Of course!" Mr. Baxter exclaimed. "Their owners didn't want them either."

"Victor, this is a lesson for Cory about love, compassion, and tenderness," she explained. Then she gave him a look and added in a slightly threatening tone, "Now, get with the program!"

Just then Cory entered, carrying Lionel. "Look at all these babes," he said to his pet. "All you have to do is pick one."

"How about Alberta?" Mrs. Baxter asked, pointing to a cage as if she were a game show hostess showing off a prize.

Cory looked at Alberta and shook his head. "She's missing her front teeth," he said. "Lionel can't wake up to that every morning.

Dad, hand me Daisy, please."

Mr. Baxter looked down at the rat nearest to him. He didn't relish having to touch it. "Tanya," he asked, "where are the rat tongs?"

"Victor," she shot back curtly. "Program."

Mr. Baxter looked at her and knew the only thing worse than touching an icky rat was dealing with an angry wife. "Fine," he answered grudgingly.

He picked up the rat named Daisy and held it as far away from his body as possible as he carried it over to Cory and Lionel.

"Have fun with Lionel," Mrs. Baxter added encouragingly. "Do your thing, girl."

"I think she just did," Mr. Baxter said as he used a tissue to wipe some rat pee from his hands.

Cory looked on as the two rats sniffed each other.

"Ooh, smells like love, huh, Lionel?" Cory said.

Even Mr. Baxter had to admit, the rats did seem to like each other.

Raven and some of the Sleevemore kids had gone out for pizza after a session at the psychic center. Raven felt bad about lying to Eddie and Chelsea, but she knew that they just wouldn't understand.

"Oh, great, a table full of kids," the waitress muttered as she walked up to the group. "What a joy."

"Raven, check this out," Carly whispered.

"Okay, make it snappy," the waitress said. "What'll it be?"

Marvin handled the ordering for the group. After all, he already knew what everyone wanted just by reading their minds.

"We'll have a small sausage and a large vegetarian," he said.

The waitress grabbed a pen with a purple

pom-pom at the end and wrote down the order. Then she tucked it behind her right ear.

"You know, on second thought," Marvin said, "I want to change that."

This time, Carly used her powers to make the pen float up in the air above the waitress's head. It spun around and around as the waitress patted her hair and behind both ears, searching frantically for her pen.

Finally Carly put the pen on the waitress's head, so it was sticking straight up.

"Did anyone see my—" the waitress asked.

The kids all pointed to the top of her head simultaneously. The waitress retrieved the pen with a puzzled look.

"My lucky pen," the waitress said, oblivious to what was going on. "I'd hate to lose that."

The waitress rushed back to the kitchen, muttering to herself. Carly used her telekinesis to lift the waitress's wig off her head. It hovered in the air for a moment. Then it followed her into the kitchen.

"You guys are so wrong," Raven said, unable to hold back her laughter.

Marvin smiled. He was having a great time. "It's so easy to goof on the normies," he said.

"Normies?" Raven asked.

"That's what we call nonpsychics behind their backs," Carly explained.

"As in, how many normies does it take to change a lightbulb?" Marvin asked.

Raven thought for a moment. "I give up."

"One," Marvin said with a laugh. "But he doesn't do it till after it burns out."

Raven and the others all burst out laughing.

"I get it," she said. "'Cause they can't see into the future like—" She thought for a moment. "My friends would totally not get that."

"That's why it's way more fun to hang out

with your own kind," Carly said.

Suddenly Raven stopped laughing. Chelsea and Eddie might not get an inside joke about being psychic, but they were her crew. Her best friends.

"Oh, I have fun with my friends," she told them. "It's just that, sometimes, they just don't understand what I'm going through."

"The normie problem. We've all been through it," Marvin told her.

"Whoa," Raven said, getting a jolt of psychic energy. "I think I'm feeling something."

"Is it a vision?" Carly asked, eager to see another display of Raven's powers.

Raven thought for a moment. It wasn't really a vision. "More like a vibe," she explained.

Carly was still excited. "That's what we were working on in the lab today," she said. "Just go with it."

Raven closed her eyes and concentrated as

hard as she could. "I see two people," she said. She kept concentrating. "I can't make them out, but they're very angry."

She thought some more but couldn't figure it all out. "But who are they?" she asked.

Just then she opened her eyes and saw the answer standing in front of her: Chelsea and Eddie, looking none too happy.

Uh-oh, Raven thought.

"Hey, Raven," Chelsea said. "How's the rat?"

Chapter Five

"So, you met some kids who are psychic," Chelsea said. "Why'd you have to blow us off?"

"And lie to us?" added Eddie. "What's up with that?"

Raven, Chelsea, and Eddie had gone to another table. Raven knew she had some explaining to do—and fast.

"I just didn't know if you guys would click with them," Raven tried to explain. "You guys like to bowl; they . . ."

She motioned over to the Sleevemore kids and saw that Carly was using her telekinetic powers to shake some hot pepper onto the pizza.

". . . you know, they like to defy the physical laws of the universe."

"Tell me I did not just see that," Eddie said, totally amazed.

"I know," Chelsea added. "That's a lot of pepper."

"Chelsea!" Eddie blurted. "It was floating."

"It's called telekinesis," Raven explained.

"It's still way too much pepper," Chelsea argued.

"Look, you guys have been on my case lately," Raven said, being brutally honest. "And I met some new people who really understand me and—"

"And you'd rather hang out with these freaks than us?" Eddie said.

"Freaks?" Raven was getting furious. "Is that what you call me when I'm not around?"

"He didn't mean you," Chelsea explained. "He meant them."

At the other table, Sparky had overheard Eddie's and Chelsea's remarks. He stood up, ready to use his fire-starting skills.

"Chill, Sparky," Raven said. He sat back down. Raven turned to her friends.

"You know what?" she continued. "I'm just like them. And if they're freaks, so am I!"

Raven stood up and went back to the other table with her new friends from the psychic center.

Eddie couldn't believe that Raven was ready to give up their friendship just like that.

"If she's going to be like that," he said, "let's go, Chelsea."

"Right behind you," Chelsea said. She got up dramatically and in the process hit her hand against the table.

"Oooo," she said. "I broke a nail."

"Pinkie?" Raven asked, realizing that this was the vision she had had during the volley-ball game.

"I don't even care," Chelsea said.

"Yeah, you do," Marvin blurted, reading her mind. He gave Chelsea a wink, and she ran out of the restaurant after Eddie.

Back at the Baxter house, things were going much better for Cory and his pet rat. Lionel had found his dream rat and was about to get married.

Cory had made a wedding chapel out of an old shoe box and was stylin' in a suit, complete with a flower in his lapel.

"Well, this is it, Lionel," Cory said to his rat, who was wearing a top hat and a bow tie. "You ready to tie the knot?"

Mr. and Mrs. Baxter came into the room. Like Cory, they were all dressed up for the wedding. Mr. Baxter had on a gray suit with a flower in his lapel, and Mrs. Baxter wore an elegant dress and flowers in her hair.

"I can't believe you're making me wear a suit to this thing," Mr. Baxter said.

Mrs. Baxter gave him a disapproving look. "It's a wedding."

He shot a look right back at her. Was his whole family crazy? "They're rats."

"They're in love," she responded.

His look didn't change. Neither did his answer. "They're rats."

Cory placed Lionel at the front of the chapel.

Mr. Baxter lifted Daisy, complete with a white veil, out of a covered box. He set her down in the aisle of the cardboard chapel.

Cory pressed a button, and "Here Comes the Bride" started playing on the CD player.

Daisy ran up the aisle next to Lionel.

Mrs. Baxter smiled as though she were at an actual wedding. "Honey, doesn't Daisy look beautiful?"

Cory put a tiny book on the pulpit and

began to read from it as he took on the role of minister.

"We are gathered here today to join this couple in holy matrimony," he said, completely serious.

Mr. Baxter rolled his eyes, and his wife jabbed him in the stomach with her elbow.

"Lionel, Daisy," Cory continued. "I know you two are meant to be. And if your marriage is anything like my parents' marriage, then you'll be together forever."

Mr. and Mrs. Baxter glanced tenderly at each other.

"You may get mad and want to sleep on the other side of the cage," Cory added, "but hang in there. And if you ever need advice, talk to my mom and dad. 'Cause after all these years, they're still in love."

Mr. Baxter leaned his head against his wife's and they both smiled. "By the power vested in me by Norm's Pet Store," Cory said, "I now pronounce you husband and wife. Lionel, you may kiss the bride . . . or sniff her."

Lionel gave Daisy a sniff, and Mr. Baxter started crying. Marriage is a beautiful thing, he thought.

Chapter Six

The next day, Raven returned to the Sleevemore Center for more tests and exercises. She was hooked up to the oscillator, but this time it wasn't going very well at all. The other kids hovered around her as she struggled to get a vision.

"I'm seeing myself," she said, eyes closed, slowly trying to create a vision. "Surrounded by . . ." She opened her eyes and saw that the others had crowded around her a little too closely. Hello? Some personal space, please, she thought. ". . . people who really need to back up off me! All right? Okay?"

The others all took a big step back. Meanwhile, Dr. Sleevemore checked all the gauges and meters.

"You're tense and irritable and down to a one-point-six on the Sleevemore scale," he said unhappily. "This begs further study." Dr. Sleevemore ripped off a printout of the test results and headed toward his office.

"Come on, Raven," Carly said when he had gone. "It's just us now. What's up?"

"Nothing," Raven answered curtly. Just because she wasn't having a vision didn't mean something was wrong, did it?

"That's not what I'm getting," Marvin interrupted, obviously reading her mind again.

"Okay, big shot," Raven said. "You know everything. Tell me what's on my mind."

Marvin walked around the Sleevemore Cerebral Oscillator chair and concentrated. "Let's see," he said as he rubbed his temples. "You're thinking about changing shampoos."

"Wrong," Raven shot back. "It's my conditioner. Next."

Marvin thought some more. "And you miss your normie friends."

Busted, Raven thought. That was exactly what was bothering her.

"Marvin," she said, "nobody likes a show-off."

Carly understood exactly why she was so upset. "Raven, it's okay," she offered. "We all know what it's like when your friends think you're a freak."

"Actually," Raven corrected, "they think you guys are freaks."

"That is so normie," Carly responded. "But that's how they see us. That's why we have to stick together."

"I guess you're right," Raven admitted. Why couldn't all her friends get along?

"It's for the best," Carly said. "Come on. Sparky's making nachos."

She motioned across the lab to where Sparky was melting cheese with his telepathic powers. The others were dipping chips into the cheese.

"I'll get it," Marvin said.

Get what? Raven thought. Just then the doorbell rang.

Marvin opened the door, and Chelsea and Eddie walked in, looking a little nervous but determined.

Chelsea and Eddie held their hands up with their fingers in a V formation. It looked like some kind of alien salute from the movies. "We come in peace," Chelsea announced.

"Oh, boy," Marvin said, certain that this would not go well.

I can't believe they showed up here, thought Raven.

"We just want to know what's going on here," Eddie explained. "And we're not leaving until we get some . . ."

Suddenly he smelled the melting cheese and

became distracted. ". . . nachos. Until we get some nachos."

"What are you guys doing here?" Raven asked.

"Rae, we need to talk to you," Chelsea explained.

Carly came over and tried to end the conversation. "Raven, Dr. Sleevemore doesn't like visitors during research hours," she told her.

"Research?" Eddie blurted. "You're melting cheese!"

"I'll handle this," Raven assured her. Then she turned to her friends. "So you came to see the freak show?"

"I never should have said that, Rae," Eddie admitted.

"We came to apologize," said Chelsea. "We want to work things out."

"If these are your friends," Eddie said, "they're our friends, too."

"Really?" Raven asked with a smile. "You mean that?"

"Excuse me," Marvin interrupted. "Who says we want to be friends with you?"

"Excuse *me*. What's that supposed to mean?" Chelsea asked.

"It's time to leave," Carly demanded. She returned Chelsea's salute.

"And what if we don't?" Chelsea asked, standing her ground.

Ooh, my girl's getting sassy, Raven thought.

Carly looked over at a stack of doughnuts. Using her telekinetic powers, she made one of the doughnuts fly through the air and smack Eddie in the head.

"Good shot, Carly," Marvin cheered.

"So, you can throw a lousy doughnut at Eddie with your mind," countered Chelsea, not impressed.

Carly looked over and suddenly a bunch of

doughnuts flew through the air and bounced off Eddie.

Man, this is making me rethink my love of doughnuts, he thought.

"Okay, that was cool," Chelsea admitted. "But I bet you can't do it with a chair."

Carly looked over at a chair, and it started rising into the air.

"Chelsea!" Eddie shouted, more than a little worried. He didn't need her giving Carly any ideas. Being pelted with doughnuts had been bad enough.

"Okay, stop it!" Raven said firmly. She turned to Carly and the other psychics. "Those are my friends you're tele-pelting."

"*We're* your friends," Carly responded.

"Not if you can't accept Eddie and Chelsea," Raven claimed.

"Come on, Rae," Chelsea said as she took Raven by the arm. They started to leave, but

Carly wasn't about to let that happen. She focused all her psychic energy on Raven.

Chelsea tugged on Raven's arm, not understanding the holdup. "Rae?" she asked. "You coming?"

"Actually, I can't," Raven explained, unable to move her legs. "Carly?" she said, looking at her telekinetic friend.

"Raven, don't go," Carly said. "You have an amazing gift. You were making such progress here."

Eddie started pulling on Raven's arm, too. It was no use. Carly's powers were too strong.

"Hey," Eddie shouted. "If my friend wants to leave, she's leaving."

"Raven, if you leave with them, you're making a terrible mistake," said Marvin.

"The only mistake she made was coming here," countered Chelsea.

Chelsea and Eddie pulled even harder on

her arms. "Come on, Eddie," Chelsea said. "Put your back into it."

They began to get the upper hand. Carly turned to her friends.

"Guys," she said to the other psychics, "some help here."

Suddenly Raven was caught in a tug of war. Her legs floated up off the floor, and her body levitated in the air. The only thing keeping her from floating away was Chelsea and Eddie holding her arms.

"Okay," Raven shouted nervously. "Who turned off the gravity?"

"Let her go!" Carly commanded. "She belongs with us!"

"She belongs with *us*!" Eddie responded.

"I belong on the ground!" Raven shouted in desperation. "Let me go!"

Eddie and Chelsea let go, and the psychics released their concentration. Rather than fall to the ground, though, Raven started to fly across the room. She was headed right for the cerebral oscillator, when Dr. Sleevemore stepped into the room.

The doctor reached up with one hand and used his considerable psychic powers to stop Raven from crashing into the machine. "Not the oscillator," he said. "I'm still making payments."

He gently lowered Raven to the floor. Phew, that was close, Raven thought as she took a deep breath. Everyone huddled around her to see if she was all right.

"Rae, are you okay?" Chelsea asked. "Did they hurt you?"

"Us? You're the one that let go," accused Carly.

"That's what happens when you let the normies in," Marvin said matter-of-factly.

"I'd rather be a normie than a freak," Eddie countered.

"Stop!" Raven yelled. She'd had enough. She was going to make this right. "My turn! You're not a normie, and you're not a freak. We're all just people. We go to school. We hang out. We play volleyball."

"Some better than others," Chelsea corrected, still hurting from the loss of the Jefferson game.

She just wasn't gonna let that go, was she? thought Raven. "The point is, yes, I'm psychic," Raven continued, speaking to her psychic friends for a moment. "But that's not all I am. And that's not all you are either."

Carly, Marvin, and the others knew that Raven was right. But they had been hurt by too many people to accept "normies" so easily.

Raven turned to the doctor. "Dr. Sleevemore," she said, "thanks for your help, but I think it's time for me to go."

"I'm sorry to hear you say that, Raven," he

said. "But our door is always open for you."

To illustrate his point, Carly used her psychic powers to open the door.

"Thank you, Carly," Dr. Sleevemore said. Then he got a quick psychic impulse. "That's going to be the phone."

He started walking to his office, and just then the phone started to ring. Eddie and Chelsea had to admit, this was an impressive group.

"Good-bye, everyone," Raven said, and started toward the door.

Marvin stepped forward. "Look, Raven," he said. "I just wanted to say . . ."

Just then Marvin was overloaded with psychic messages he was receiving from everyone else. "Okay, okay," he told them. "Don't all think at once."

"*We*," he corrected, "all just want to say we're sorry."

Eddie looked over. He hadn't been very nice, either.

"Hey," he said, trying to make amends, "we're sorry, too."

Marvin and Eddie shook hands.

Carly smiled at Eddie and approached him. "Oh, and Eddie," she said, "yes, I'll go out with you."

Eddie was stunned. "But how did you—" Then it dawned on him. She'd read his mind. "Aaah. You got skills, girl. I like you."

Eddie smiled. But then he started to smell something weird.

"Is something burning?" he asked.

Chelsea spotted a puff of smoke coming out of the back of Eddie's pants. "I think it's you."

Eddie quickly started patting down his pants, trying to put the fire out. Carly gave Sparky a mean look.

"Sparky, we talked about this," she said.

Then she explained to Eddie, "We used to date. He's not quite over it."

"I guess he still has the *hots* for you," Chelsea said. She laughed at her joke, but the others just groaned.

Just then a doughnut flew through the air and smacked Chelsea right in the head.

"Carly?" Chelsea said with an accusing tone.

"I'm sorry, girl. That was me." Raven giggled as she licked the sugar off her fingers. She had thrown one of the leftover doughnuts at Chelsea.

Meanwhile, back at Raven's house, Mr. and Mrs. Baxter were looking at a wedding album.

"Honey, remember that?" she said, pointing to a picture of them at the altar.

Mr. Baxter nodded and thought back fondly on the day. "It was a beautiful moment."

He turned the page and started to laugh. "Look at us dancing."

"You still got the moves," his wife added.

"I hate to brag," Mr. Baxter said. "But that is a good-looking couple."

He pointed at a picture in the album. It was a heart-shaped photo of Daisy and Lionel on their big day.

Just then, Cory ran into the room, short of breath and carrying one of his rat boxes.

"Mom, Dad, congratulations," he said. "You're grandparents."

Cory opened the box to show his surprised parents. It was empty! "They were here a minute ago," he said.

Mr. and Mrs. Baxter looked at each other. It was just another crazy day in the Baxter house.

Gaze into the future and take a sneak peek at the next *That's So Raven* story. . . .

Adapted by Kimberly Morris

Based on the television series, "That's So Raven", created by Michael Poryes and Susan Sherman

Based on the episode written by Michael Feldman

Raven Baxter was a happy girl. She had on some killer jeans. Her two best friends, Chelsea Daniels and Eddie Thomas, were hangin' tight—left and right. Best of all, Devon Carter, the most gorgeous boy in San Francisco, stood less than six feet away. Life was good.

Chelsea nudged Raven with her elbow and looked sideways at Eddie. "Ooh, look, Rae. It's Devon Carter."

"Ooh, I know." Raven shot a quick glance at the divine Devon, trying not to make it obvious that she was totally crushing on him.

"So, how's it going with you two?" Eddie asked.

"Oh, great," Raven fibbed. "Things are really starting to happen between us."

Raven struck a flirty pose as Devon walked by. She struggled to keep her voice from sounding over-the-top thrilled to see him. "Hey, Devon."

"Hey, Rae." Devon gave her a shy smile, but

he didn't stop to talk. He kept on walking and opened his locker on the other side of the hall.

Raven's best friends gave her a "you wish" look.

Okay. So he wasn't exactly falling down at her feet. But in Raven's world, the glass was always half full. "See?" she said to Chelsea and Eddie. "Before it was just 'Hey.' Now it's 'Hey, *Rae.*'"

Raven believed in being positive. She was *positive* Devon was the guy for her. That had to mean he felt the same way—or would.

Eddie and Chelsea exchanged a look that said, "Poor Raven, there she goes again. Grasping at straws."

For, like, two seconds, Raven wondered if maybe they were right. Maybe she was just kidding herself. Maybe Devon wasn't interested in her at all.

But then she felt the noisy hall grow silent. Time seemed to stand still.

Through her eye
The vision runs
Flash of future
Here it comes—

I see Devon surrounded by a dreamy light. I see his face moving closer to mine. Closer . . . closer . . . closer . . .

Behind him I see . . . a giant teddy bear and a robot.

A GIANT TEDDY BEAR AND A ROBOT???

How weird is that?

Raven snapped back to the present. She'd just had a premonition that Devon was going to kiss her. Did it get any better than this?

"Devon Carter is gonna kiss me!" she shrieked happily.

Some of the kids walking near Raven stopped in their tracks and stared at her as if she'd lost her mind.

Uh-oh! She was making a total fool of herself. "It's my favorite song," Raven added quickly. "'Devon Carter's gonna kiss me, gonna kiss me,'" she improvised, trying to make it sound like she was singing some hit tune.

But Chelsea knew exactly what Raven had said. She also knew her best friend was psychic. She clutched Raven's sleeve. "Wait, Devon Carter is going to kiss you? When?"

"I don't know." Raven was so excited, she could hardly stand still. "But there was a robot and a giant teddy bear standing right behind him."

"What were they doing, lining up?" Eddie cracked.

"Ooh, Rae, you should ask him out," Chelsea urged. "I mean Devon Carter, not the teddy bear or the robot."

Raven suddenly felt shy. "Nuh-uh."

"Yeah," Chelsea insisted.

"No way."

"C'mon."

"Uh-uh. You think?" Raven asked.

Chelsea's raised eyebrows challenged her. "Yeah." Chelsea nodded, looking across the hall. Devon had just closed his locker and was heading off to class. It was now or never.

Raven took a deep breath and started toward him. But then she chickened out. She whipped back around to face Chelsea. "You know, I was just thinking . . ."

She was stalling for time. But Chelsea and Eddie weren't going to let her get away with it. Together, they pushed her in Devon's direction. "Just go!" Eddie insisted.

Raven lurched toward Devon. He looked up and smiled. Luckily, she got her balance back before she fell right into him. "Oh, hey, Devon. Hey, hey," she babbled. "Hi, how you doin'?"

Devon smiled uncertainly and waited for her to get to the point.

"I was just wondering, if you're not doing anything this Friday, maybe you and me . . . I . . . you and I . . . We . . ." Raven lost her nerve and trailed off.

Devon finished the sentence for her. ". . . We could hang out?"

"Okay. I'd love to, thanks for asking," Raven said happily. Wow! she thought. The boy was smooth. He knew how to help a lady in distress.

"I'll call you," Devon said, ambling down the hallway.

Raven gave him a little wave. "Okay, I'll be

waiting . . . by the phone so patiently," she added in a small voice when he was out of earshot.

Raven hurried back to Chelsea and Eddie. What great buds. She would never have had the nerve to ask Devon out. All she'd needed was a little push. And they had given it to her. Literally.

"Okay, what'd he say, what'd he say?" Chelsea asked. "Tell me what he said."

"It's on for Friday. Just Devon and me . . . and a robot and a teddy bear. It's going to be so romantic!" Raven threw her arms open— *whap! whap!*—accidentally smacking her friends and sending them sprawling.

After school, Raven did her best to beat Cory through the back door of the Baxters' house. Her master plan was to lock him out and hope he would run away and get lost.

Unfortunately, Cory poured on some last-minute speed and made it through the door, almost stepping on Raven's heels.

"Why do you always have to follow me?" Raven groaned as she put her books down on the kitchen counter.

"I was using your big head to block out the sun," Cory said.

Raven gave him a withering look. "Well, you know what? It was cute when you were born and when Mom and Dad brought you home from the hospital, but you're still here."

Cory's sour smile said, "You're so funny—not."

The phone rang. Raven immediately forgot about Cory and dove for the phone. It might be Chelsea. Better yet, it might be Devon.

But Cory's grubby little hand closed over the handset first. Before Raven could stop him, he was doing his pesky little-brother thing.

"Baxter residence," he cooed in his pretend-sweet voice. "Cute one speaking. . . . Devon?"

Raven lunged for the phone, but Cory jumped out of reach. "Sorry, Raven's plucking her mustache right now."

Raven managed to grab Cory. "Give me that!" she snapped. She ripped the phone away, composed her face, and then spoke. "Hey, Devon."

Cory grabbed a bowl of grapes. Raven ignored him. She was not going to let her little gargoyle of a brother distract her while she made plans with Devon. Even the sound of his voice made her heart beat faster.

"Hey, Raven. The reason I called is, I can't hang out with you Friday night."

Raven's heart sank. Oh no! Cory began pelting her with grapes. Raven picked up a skillet from the counter and batted them away like tennis balls. "No! Why not?"

"I'm sorry, but I promised to take my little sister to Pizza Pals."

Cory threw another handful of grapes. Raven dodged them and tried to sound cool, calm, and collected. "Pizza Pals? What's Pizza Pals?"

"You know, the pizza place for kids," Devon explained. "They've got these crazy characters, like a robot and a giant teddy bear."

Cory ran around behind Raven. She could feel grapes bouncing off the back of her jacket. But who cared?

A robot and a teddy bear! Cory and his grubby grapes disappeared. All Raven could see was the image in her vision. She remembered seeing Devon lean toward her—*with a robot and a teddy bear behind him*!

Fate! Fate! Fate! It was all adding up. Things were falling into place.

"I am so there!" Raven shrieked happily.

"What?" Devon asked.

Cory moved in for another grape attack. Raven reached out, grabbed the top of his head, and pulled him in close. Then she wrapped her arm around his neck and grabbed him in a headlock.

She looked down into his big brown eyes and thought, if you didn't really know Cory—which Devon didn't—you might actually think he was a nice little kid instead of a troll. "I mean, Devon, hey, you've got a little sister, and guess what? I have a little brother. So, you know, we could get them together."

Cory struggled, but Raven held on tight.

"Sounds cool," Devon said. "Because Nadine and I are really close. I think that's so important."

"So do I. In fact, my brother and I, we couldn't be much closer." She squashed Cory's face against her shoulder.

"Cool," said Devon.

"Yeah, so, anyway," Raven said, "we'll see you Friday night at Pizza Pals. Okay?"

"Later."

"All right. Bye, Devon." Raven disconnected the phone and allowed Cory to escape.

"No 'we' won't," Cory insisted, twisting away.

Raven spoke in a loving voice. "Cory, you know how Mom and Dad are always telling us that one day we're going to need each other?" Her eyes turned hard and determined. "That day is here," she announced.

"Then it's going to be a very expensive day for you," Cory warned, his brown eyes turning even harder and more determined than Raven's.

a comedy of
psychic proportions!
that's so raven
every day on
Disney Channel!
Disney Channel
original
DisneyChannel.com

The new book series.
Available wherever books are sold.

W.i.t.c.h.

Will   Irma   Taranee   Cornelia   Hay Lin

The magic of friendship

Collect them all!

Make some powerful friends at www.clubwitch.com

HYPERION
BOOKS FOR CHILDREN

Betty & Veronica

Betty and Veronica wear the latest fashions, know what's cool, and are always up for some fun. Now they are telling all to their fans! Full of humor and attitude, these books will show you how to deal with everything from school to boys—all from the perspective of two famous and fabulous best friends . . . and crush rivals!

Available wherever books are sold!

For more fun with Archie and the gang, log onto www.archiecomics.com.